The Greatest Match Ever

FRANK Z. LLOBERA

Copyright © 2024 Frank Z. Llobera

All rights reserved. No part of this book may be reproduced,
or stored in a retrieval system, or transmitted
in any form or by any means, electronic, mechanical,
photocopying, recording, or otherwise, without express
written permission of the author. All photographic content in
this publication is the exclusive property of the author.

ISBN: 9798322047223

The Greatest Match Ever

"If you can dream—and not make dreams your master;
If you can think—and not make thoughts your aim;
If you can meet with Triumph and Disaster
And treat those two impostors just the same."

—RUDYARD KIPLING

CONTENTS

PRELUDE 7

D-DAY MINUS ONE 11

D-DAY 25

AFTERWORD 63

ACKNOWLEDGEMENT

Special thanks to everyone mentioned in this story, whose involvement made for a truly unforgettable experience.

PRELUDE

In one of the most iconic finals in tennis history, the Spaniard Rafael Nadal engaged in a memorable battle against the Swiss maestro Roger Federer at the 2008 Wimbledon Championships. The match kept spectators on the edge of their seats as both rivals fought for victory.

Spanning almost five hours, the thriller was interrupted twice by rain, further adding to the suspense and drama. Indeed, the impression was that the game might go on endlessly, and perhaps it was this marriage of epic and mystique that led pundits to label this final as "The greatest match ever."

Whilst the sports chronicle of this game is familiar to

many, I find myself in a position to narrate it from a different angle. The perspective of an ordinary fan who was in Wimbledon on that fateful day. The viewpoint of those who lacked the money to purchase individual tickets—costing hundreds or thousands of pounds—and may have attempted to gain entry at the eleventh hour, or catch a glimpse of the final upon the branches of a towering tree; oblivious, in any case, to the rites and secrets confined within the sanctuary of world tennis and sport, known as Wimbledon.

Now, I shall endeavour to be your guide throughout these pages. Being someone who leans more towards literature than sports, nonetheless, destiny did cast me upon the grounds of Wimbledon on that day, July 6, 2008.

Little did I anticipate that the match would reach legendary status.

Greetings and welcome to London, SW19.

D-DAY MINUS ONE

14:30

Call me Frank. Some years ago, having little or no money in my purse, and being in my early twenties—nostalgic for my native island of Mallorca, juggling studies and trainee roles in Dublin and in London—I was given the opportunity to witness a temporary fusion of the English and Spanish idiosyncrasies, all motivated by circumstances other than travel or tourism.

Undoubtedly, I speak of that summer in 2008, when the match that was hailed as the greatest of all time unfolded at the home of British tennis, The All England Lawn Tennis and Croquet Club.

Through the whims of fortune, I was in London back then. And so, I found myself stumbling upon the chance to accompany a friend on an expedition to attend the 2008 Wimbledon Championships Men's Singles final between Roger Federer and Rafael Nadal. It was scheduled for Sunday, July 6.

For three consecutive years, the Swiss ace Roger Federer and the young Spaniard Rafael Nadal had held the ATP World No. 1 and No. 2 rankings, cultivating a rivalry that gripped audiences across the globe. With each summer came the showdowns, as they challenged each other's dominance on the courts of Paris and London.

Our journey commenced the previous day, on Saturday, July 5. It was a moderately sunny afternoon in London, which certainly didn't foreshadow the foul weather we would wake up to on Sunday. Or at least I thought so. A rookie's mistake, for any seasoned Londoner understands the random nature of the city's climate. In truth, it usually inclines towards deterioration—but at the time, I was unaware of that, having spent most of my childhood and adolescence in Mallorca, like Rafael Nadal.

Now, making our way to The All England Lawn

Tennis and Croquet Club, we had to take a tour of London, courtesy of the generally unpredictable public transportation system.

The team embarking on this tennis odyssey thus consisted of two persons: Sergio and myself. He was a spirited fellow from Asturias, Spain, in his late twenties, employed at a hotel in London. Sergio, a devoted aficionado of football and tennis, had even ventured into the realms of journalism at Spain's *"Diario Marca"* for a spell.

We had arranged to meet at 2:30 p.m. at my student flat near Camden Town. Upon Sergio's arrival, we set off laden with a bunch of stuff and suitcases—not towards the grounds of Wimbledon, but towards Old Street—to my freshly rented accommodation.

Let it be known that I took advantage of Sergio's help to conclude the move of some of my belongings and other items to my new abode. This followed a tumultuous incident involving my flatmates, six persons of different temperaments and backgrounds.

In brief, the conflict exploded during our search for improved lodging. As our current rental contract neared its end, we committed to a flat in the suburban reaches of

London, in Wood Green. Yet, at the eleventh hour, it suddenly dawned on some of us that the house, its location, the commute, and the company weren't worth it. Hence, we abruptly chose to part ways, sparking discord amongst the other flatmates who were more determined and had even begun planning a housewarming party. I harbour no regrets—I wasn't the main culprit for the breaking of this fellowship, and I believe it simply wasn't meant to be.

Let's not veer off course anyway. I was now eagerly anticipating the adventure ahead, viewing our Wimbledon escapade as an opportunity to evade the woes of my student life.

Around 4 p.m. we concluded the removal job, and set off towards the southwesterly parts of London—towards Wimbledon, SW19.

With eagerness and anticipation, Sergio uttered an obscure Spanish idiom, which could be freely translated in English as:

"Off we go, from Scylla to Charybdis!"

And from Old Street we descended into the Tube. Initially, boarding the Northern Line, we transferred to yet another Northern Line segment (sounds peculiar if you aren't a Londoner, I know), and our journey then led us to the District Line. We got off at St James's Park, making our way to the home of Arnaud, a friend of mine who was working at an American investment bank.

It was just a pit stop, and our purpose was clear: to borrow two sleeping bags and a tent he had used whilst travelling in the Atlas Mountains—or perhaps it was in the Himalayas or other remote places.

As Sergio and I stepped into the brand-new apartment, which was located near the Houses of Parliament, we were greeted by Arnaud. Following a convivial conversation, he kindly provided us with the camping package.

"Cheers! Wish us luck!" said I, as we finally set out on our adventure towards Wimbledon.

Upon exiting Arnaud's and his colleagues' apartment, I sensed a mix of admiration and envy on Sergio's face.

"Arnaud's apartment is bloody brilliant, isn't it?" said I.

"Well, my flat ain't so bad, but it could be much better," said Sergio.

"Same. You just saw it."

"Are we jealous, Frank? Well, a healthy feeling of envy doesn't exist. So, I've to admit that I wish the worst to

Arnaud and his pals."

"Don't be mean," said I, laughing. "I actually stayed here for a few weeks when I first moved to London."

We headed back to St James's Park tube station, boarding the District Line bound for Wimbledon, destination Southfields Station. Seemingly, we needn't disembark at the Wimbledon Station, which comes afterwards, to get to the domains of The All England Lawn Tennis and Croquet Club.

Regardless, we reached SW19. Anticipation hung thick in the air like a heavy mist.

Triumph and Disaster awaited us...

Yet, our aim was clear. To pitch Arnaud's tent near the fortified premises of Wimbledon, and gain entry within its walls by daybreak—an enterprise as evident as the rising sun.

18:00

We marched on, reaching the grounds that functioned as a designated parking area, marked as Car Park 10—a location now engraved in our memories.

That's where we were about to camp, near the beginning of the queue leading to the ground level entrance. The site was therefore a makeshift parking lot, nestled amidst much fallow land, and with booths positioned in front of the Wimbledon fortress.

To our surprise, we observed that there were hardly any tents and realised that our entry into the premises of Wimbledon was going to be assured the next day, barring any major catastrophe.

Much ado about nothing? We arrived a full day ahead of the final, anticipating a quite bustling scene, yet the reality fell far short of our expectations.

We couldn't help it, so we set up the tent and ventured out to explore the surroundings. Security guards kept an eye over the tents but prompted us to lock our valuables and leave the remaining bags and belongings inside our tent.

To pamper ourselves, we bought a few beers and chips, costing 8 pounds in total.

Back to base camp, we engaged in conversation with a family hailing from Newcastle—a mother accompanied by her two daughters. They regaled us tales of their tennis adventures and their attendance at matches during this tournament, featuring both rising stars and seasoned champions: Novak Djokovic, Andy Murray, Serena Williams, Venus Williams, Marat Safin, and the like.

Ah! And let's not forget about Phil, the quintessential tennis enthusiast, a camper who had endured the elements for a staggering ten consecutive days.

Adorned with an array of wristbands granting access to various courts, the veteran Mr. Phil Philanthropist was an icon in the community, revered by the Wimbledon queue-dwellers who greeted him with admiration.

Obviously, he felt at home, navigating the grounds with ease, continuously talking to the stewards and fellow fans.

20:00

The stewards approached and handed us vouchers, confirming our admission status, 6th and 7th in the queue.

"This is it," said we. "Wimbledon, let's go!"

Additionally, we were provided with a guide, as

remarkable as it was surprising, detailing the intricacies of queuing for entry at Wimbledon. "A Guide for Queuing at Wimbledon," read the title that might have belonged in a Julio Cortázar surrealist short story. All in all, it was a 20-page brochure in vibrant colours.

"If you can wait and not be tired by waiting," I pondered, inspired by Rudyard Kipling.

Night descended gradually and the chill of evening enveloped us. We turned to our provisions for solace—especially the four suits: clubs, hearts, diamonds, and spades.

You've guessed it, we engaged in a round of card games between phone calls to friends, enjoying a snack of Quely biscuits and Iberian chorizo—a synthesis of Mallorcan and Asturian flavours.

Supper over, we retired to rest, mindful that the wake-up call awaited us before the break of dawn, around 6 a.m.

Tranquillity and comfort eluded me throughout the night. I rolled about a great deal, and couldn't sleep for a long time. The early reveille wasn't the only contributing factor, though it certainly had an impact. Rather, the discomfort was deepened by the infernal terrain and the lack of a ground mat.

In short, the night would pass in a cycle of dozing and awakening. Despite it all, I said to myself, "Mind over matter, no complaining," knowing that tomorrow was holding the promise of enjoyment, and perchance glory.

Picture: Rafael Nadal training on Court 19, Wimbledon

D-DAY

5:45

Drums of war resonated in the vicinity of SW19. The martial stewards played reveille.

Sergio woke up instantly. Might I even add that he sprang up nanoseconds later, as if triggered by an electrical switch?

Indeed, one could sense the excitement in his drowsy visage. It was a culmination of improbable events. His home team Sporting de Gijón rising to Primera División of LaLiga, Spain's triumph in the UEFA Euro 2008, and now the 2008 Wimbledon final—a sports aficionado from

Asturias couldn't have asked for more. Having stormed Trafalgar Square under Nelson's astonished gaze during the celebrations of the UEFA Euro 2008, he was now prepared to venture into the heart of Wimbledon.

I, conversely, no matter how motivated I was, lingered in bed for as long as I could. *Nihil sub sole novum,*[1] and laziness got the better of me. Also, after such a restless sleep, it was a struggle to get up from my cot.

With lightning speed, then, we dismantled the tent, stowed away some of our belongings, and voilà! We plunged straight into our allotted place in the Wimbledon queue.

The atmosphere was buzzing with excitement. Suddenly, a busload of expeditioners pulled up. A frenzy ensued as everyone scrambled to secure their spot in the queue.

It was at that moment when the most ceremonious steward appeared. His smile was beaming as he shouted something along the lines of, "Let's start moving, ladies and gentlemen."

And just as in a military parade, he assumed control of the entire queue, dictating the pace and direction,

---

[1] "Nothing new under the sun," in Latin.

marching briskly towards the gates of The All England Lawn Tennis and Croquet Club.

This may seem like an exaggeration; nevertheless, I felt the only thing missing was the Pomp and Circumstance March.

For those unfamiliar with the Wimbledon Championships, it's difficult to grasp just how formal the tournament is, imbued with traditions and features. Queuing up is just one of numerous rituals, alongside players dressing almost entirely in white, minimal advertising, no matches scheduled on the Middle Sunday,[2] and so on. Whilst it might appear irritating to some, these customs remain integral to the tournament's unique charm and prestige.

Eventually, we arrived at the main entrance, only to encounter an unexpected barrier. The steward said:

"This is the end of the queue, ladies and gentlemen. We've got a bit of a wait ahead—three hours until we open our doors at 10 a.m."

---

[2] Recently, the All England Lawn Tennis Club decided to eliminate the Middle Sunday rest day.

7:00

"Three hours. Did I hear it correctly?"

"Yes," said Sergio, "from 7 to 10 a.m."

Such was the case. The never-ending saga.

"If you can wait and not be tired by waiting," I reiterated.

My sensations were mixed. In moments like these, I couldn't help but question the sanity of our actions. Was our awaiting zeal justified, or had this tennis expedition crossed the threshold from enthusiasm to fanaticism?

We had heard before of people camping out at Wimbledon just to gain entry, or individuals paying exorbitant sums to witness a single match; and it had all seemed absurd to us at the time.

Yet here we were, Sergio and I, having not only camped but also willing to pay a small fortune to attend the final—a fortune we lacked, mind you, and in any case the Centre Court was sold out.

Putting aside these deliberations, our main preoccupation was the prospect of filling the next three hours. It was also then that we acknowledged the value of the folding chairs brought along by Phil and other tennis aficionados, who were stationed along the Wimbledon queue like relaxed residents on the streets of Deià or Valldemossa, in Mallorca.

The sun, meanwhile, played hide-and-seek behind shifting clouds, followed by rain, then wind, then a return of sunlight accompanied by an unexpected chill, only to be followed again by rain... I wasn't used to such erratic weather patterns in the summer over a single three-hour span.

What a shame no one captured a photo of us during that moment. Picture this: Sergio and I ridiculously sprawled on the grass, his Spanish flag draped from our feet to our knees, my jacket covering our legs, and an umbrella precariously perched above our heads like a makeshift hat, shielding our torsos and faces from the occasional downpour.

Around 9 o'clock, the weather took a turn for the better, and we found ourselves listening to the tales of a Canadian supporter. She was a merry young woman, telling first-hand accounts of feats she had witnessed at the US Open, the French Open, and the Wimbledon

Championships. One could surmise that Australia was a destination she had in mind.

We also conversed with other fans, who exuded passion for tennis. Truly, we were surrounded by the most devoted tennis aficionados, people who paid scant attention to nationalities or flags and focused only on the love for the game.

10:00

It felt like an eternity had passed when an announcement blared over the megaphone.

"Access to the venue is now open."

Madness ensued. Everyone hastily collected their belongings and rushed in a stampede towards the entrance.

"It's every man for himself," said Sergio.

And apparently, all semblance of order had dissolved; there were no more hierarchies in the queue. We were now in the jungle, and several people surged past us.

However, all efforts were futile. Again, we found

ourselves in another queue, awaiting security checks akin to those at airports. The process was straightforward but time-consuming: passing through weapon and metal detectors, undergoing X-ray scans of our belongings, etcetera.

Oh, and they confiscated the Spanish flag that Sergio carried, citing security reasons. He protested vigorously, but eventually surrendered to avoid expulsion.

10:30

We had passed the security controls. Sergio's indignation was palpable following the incident with the flag. I tried my best not to laugh.

After navigating through yards and yards of stairs and greenery, we finally entered the premises of Wimbledon.

But hold on! Another queue awaited us to access a fenced-off area. To make matters worse, we had been overtaken by about a hundred people due to the flag incident, which we had to store in a locker for the non-refundable fee of one pound.

As the drizzle fell, we finally reached the ticket booths. Eight quid cost the entrance.

We coughed up the money, and there we were, in Tennisland London. Would those eight pounds be the best we'd ever spent?

10:45

Sergio's indignation vanished in an instant upon entering the main grounds.

After sixteen hours of enduring various incidents, queues, light showers, and chilly winds, we finally made it inside.

First impressions flooded in as we entered The All England Lawn Tennis and Croquet Club, which felt like a tennis-themed amusement park. It evoked memories of my childhood trip to Disneyland Paris in 1998 just before the FIFA World Cup. These blurry memories, I presumed, would still linger in my memory for years to come, probably superseded by those from Wimbledon 2008.

"Green, how I love you, green," said I, quoting

Federico García Lorca's poem.

Green everywhere. Green courts, and green roofs. Green, how I love you, green!

As we entered, we caught sight of the distant Centre Court, flanked by No. 1 Court. There were stalls exhibiting souvenirs, booklets, and assorted merchandise; whilst the iconic Wimbledon draw boards displayed the singles and doubles players, their results, and the order of play for all courts.

Excited for the match due to start at 14:00, we began exploring the grounds, making a quick stop at the Wimbledon Store—let's not dwell on the extent of our eventual spending there.

11:15

"Toni!"

We had just laid eyes on Rafael Nadal's uncle and main coach, Toni Nadal, but it all happened in a split second.

I had heard Mallorcan dialect being spoken, shouted from a side door of the Centre Court to someone in the media area. We thought that it could only be people from Nadal's team.

And so, his coach Toni Nadal and assistant Carlos Costa, the latter a Catalan tennis player from the early 1990s, briefly appeared in the vicinity before vanishing again.

It seemed we had missed the chance to capture a few good pictures, as we failed to act promptly and draw our weapons in time—a far cry from the skills of my great-uncle, the RAF pilot William Watson Ritchie, who fought in World War II and was later promoted to Air Commodore. Following retirement, he pursued a career as a sculptor in Palma de Mallorca.

Turning our attention back to Nadal's camp, they were focused on the imminent challenge, getting ready for the final showdown.

The 2008 Wimbledon Championships Men's Singles final marked the third consecutive year in which Federer and Nadal met in the Wimbledon final. Roger Federer was the ATP World No. 1, and he had won not only both previous encounters but had been the reigning Wimbledon champion since 2003. Thus, Federer was aiming for a record sixth consecutive title; he was playing to make history.

The stakes were high, and the coaches' enterprise was anything but simple. They needed to guide Rafael Nadal, the King of Clay, to a long-awaited triumph on the grass courts of Wimbledon, also known as Roger Federer's garden.

Meanwhile, my preoccupations appeared trivial. In jest, I found myself wondering if the world had been turned upside down. Were Mallorcan visitors supposed to be found in London in the middle of summer? Wasn't it supposed to be the other way around?

11:30

We continued our exploration, retracing our steps towards the Centre Court, when suddenly, we noticed a crowd gathering in the spot where we had seen Toni Nadal earlier.

This time it was Rafa, though we only realised it later, as he was surrounded by fans.

Instead, we caught Toni Nadal's attention.

Upon hearing a fellow Mallorcan—in London, it's like finding a needle in a haystack—he paused, allowing us to snap a few photos together. He also mentioned that they were about to head for a pre-match training session on Court 19. Sergio, deftly, took the chance to strike up a conversation with Toni as we made our way there.

Court 19 was small and only boasted three rows of seats. Despite being the last ones, Sergio and I asserted ourselves and claimed seats in the front row, invoking the law of the jungle.

The ticket price had long been amortised. Still, observing the ATP World No. 2 player Rafael Nadal training with Carlos Costa just a few yards away was nothing short of spectacular.

For those who may not be tennis experts, let me assure you, the balls Nadal was striking resembled missiles. It may not appear so on television, but up close, they seemed nearly impossible to return. Also owing to the characteristics of the grass surface, the tennis ball barely bounced, and Carlos Costa struggled to keep up, clearly overwhelmed by the shots from his friend Rafa.

Hence, I could somewhat envision what it might have been like to witness the match in the Centre Court.

Because if Rafael Nadal's shots were powerful, Roger Federer didn't lag behind with his targeted projectiles.

The drizzle returned. The training session concluded as the rain intensified.

At that moment, Rafael Nadal headed towards our sector of Court 19, as it provided the closest exit. Immediately, the crowd surged, clamouring for autographs, pictures, and reaching out to touch him as if he were the Pope.

Rafa seemed completely absorbed and focused on the final against the ATP World No. 1 player. He signed one or two tennis balls for the fans, a gesture of great generosity given that it's not customary before such a high-stakes match. Regarding photos, he only agreed to one, though it didn't turn out well, as I can personally attest.

Let me outline what occurred. Rafael Nadal passed by us, and I said to him in Mallorcan dialect:

"Rafael, can we take a photo?"

Nadal muttered: "Quickly, please!"

And amidst the sea of spectators, I snapped two selfies, each one worse than the other, wishing him, "Good luck!" as he departed. And so, our paths and destinies united if only for a fleeting moment.

Moments later, some French teenagers, mostly fans of Roger Federer, approached us, curious why Rafael Nadal had only taken a photo with us.

I countered, in French:

"*Nous sommes les meilleurs.*"

We were the best, so to speak.

All kidding aside, Rafa had noticed my accent. However, the rain was pouring down, and I had lost sight of Sergio, who dashed away like lightning, chasing the Spanish champion. So, I didn't delve too deeply into explaining this issue to them. We still had a brief conversation about tennis, notwithstanding my mediocre French.

Later, I considered the matter a moment. What a Jungian synchronicity it was for members of the Nadal family from Manacor and the Llobera family from Can Aulí, Pollença, to encounter each other in London on a summer day in 2008. Indeed, what could have been more Mallorcan in London than a conjunction of the Nadal and Llobera dynasties?

Perhaps an *ensaimada* filled with *sobrasada*.

13:00

Rain fell tirelessly, serving as a reminder of who was the Supreme Commander of the Wimbledon's Championships.

We took advantage of the unceasing shower to explore both the Centre Court and No. 1 Court. The guards, in a commendable gesture, allowed us entry to snap some photos—a surprising act, considering the security measures we had encountered earlier.

With great interest, we visited the hall decorated with portraits of past champions, and found the splendid verses of Rudyard Kipling, from his poem "If—."

Two verses stood in capital letters, resonating within the confines of Wimbledon:

IF YOU CAN MEET WITH TRIUMPH AND DISASTER
AND TREAT THOSE TWO IMPOSTORS JUST THE SAME.

And indeed, this is what would occur to the two champs over the course of the five sets of that match.

Federer.

Nadal.

Triumph.

Disaster.

In no order.

14:35

At last, the match commenced.[3]

The players were scheduled to be on court at 14:00, but the start of the match was delayed by 35 minutes due to rain.

We had settled on the Aorangi Terrace, known as Henman Hill. It was a place for the masses without show court tickets, featuring a giant screen adjacent to No. 1 Court—a scene that I had previously glimpsed on television. Nonetheless, I couldn't have imagined that one day I would be there, amongst a thousand devoted

---

[3] Note that this tournament was a Grand Slam event and thus the men played best-of-five sets—meaning they needed to win three out of five sets to secure victory.

spectators.

The match unfolded amidst anticipation, and applause was shared between Roger Federer and Rafael Nadal, albeit with varying enthusiasm, echoing the ebbs and flows of the match.

In the early stages of the first set, Rafael Nadal broke Roger Federer's serve, establishing a 3–1 lead. Sustaining his strong performance, a hungry Nadal went on to claim the first set with a score of 6–4.[4]

Although this wasn't entirely unexpected, Nadal wasn't considered the top favourite for the Wimbledon final, as mentioned before.

The weather, far from sunny, was quite gloomy, yet the first and second sets proceeded without interruption. As the clouds thickened, a biting breeze also set in, courtesy of the British summer.

Much to mine and everyone's surprise, Rafael Nadal maintained his stellar performance and successfully

---

[4] For those unaccustomed with tennis rules, a set is won by the first player achieving six games, with a margin of at least two games over the other side (e.g., 6–4 or 6–3). If the score happens to be tied at 5–5 (5 games each), a player needs to clinch two consecutive games to claim the set. In the event of a 6–6 tie, a tiebreaker game is played to determine the set's outcome.

secured the second set 6–4 after winning five consecutive games, having trailed 1–4, and showing notable mental strength.

"In Nadal we trust," we had said optimistically before the match.

However, in spite of Nadal's two-sets-to-love lead and needing just one more set to secure victory, I actually struggled to believe it.

Be that how it may, Federer found himself in a quite precarious situation. He faced the uphill task of winning the next three sets to achieve his comeback.

Failure to do so would usher in a new Wimbledon champion for the first time since 2003.

16:15

The battle continued, as Roger Federer fought back, determined not to lose. It was at that moment he realized he was the five-time defending champion. What's more, he was playing on grass.

A dangerous moment for the Swiss arrived in the third

set when, tied at 3–3, Nadal earned a triple break point—a huge chance to break Federer's serve, provided he converted one of the three chances.

However, Federer showcased his brilliance and tenacity, rallying to claim five consecutive points and thwarting the direst of situations, setting the score at 4–3 in the third set.

"Go, Roger!" cried out his supporters, back from the dead.

Their faith was growing stronger in the hopes of extending the final.

"What's your take on the fateful match that's currently taking place in Wimbledon?" I asked, in the manner of an announcer.

"I just hope it doesn't rain," said he, sternly.

16:50

Yet, minutes later, it started raining. It was a crucial moment, with Federer leading in the third set 5–4.

Drizzle came and went, and Wimbledon court

attendants were prompted to cover the delicate grass. The match was suspended—a massive blow for all spectators.

We had no choice but to leave Henman Hill, embarking on another exploration of the Wimbledon grounds.

As we leisurely strolled near the Centre Court, we came across an unexpected familiar face, known for his support of Rafael Nadal.

It was the president at the time of Real Madrid, Mr. Ramón Calderón.

He was engaging in a casual conversation, chatting with his brother and two other gentlemen in suits who appeared to be either executives or members of Madrid's high society.

Sergio hesitated for a moment, but obviously, he wasn't going to miss the opportunity to strike up a conversation.

"Excuse me, uh... Don Ramón, two *madridistas* here," said Sergio.

It should be clarified that the fans of Real Madrid Football Club were in actuality Sergio and Mr. Calderón himself.

"Hey, how are you? What are you doing in London? Did you come from Spain to see Rafa?" said he, very politely.

"No, not really, we're working in London."

His brother seemingly murmured something to him. Mr. Calderón asked us:

"So, what's the talk in England about Cristiano Ronaldo?"

"Well, they're worried he'll leave Manchester United," said Sergio.

"We'll bring him to Madrid anyway. Don't worry."

And so, it appears Mr. Calderón wasn't bluffing. Then, his brother snapped a photo of the three of us.

18:10

The sun was returning, and an 80-minute interruption due to rain came to an end. The score stood at 6–4, 6–4, 4–5, with Nadal maintaining the lead overall.

The players were greeted back with a thunderous ovation, and Swiss maestro Roger Federer got down to work following the rain interruption.

Diving into the matter, he won the third set in the

tiebreaker—thus resulting in a final score of 7–6.[5]

Sergio remained sombre as the crowd erupted in applause. Was the tide turning against my compatriot Rafael Nadal?

It appeared so, and the atmosphere was fraught with tension.

18:50

The fourth set unfolded with unparalleled intensity. A symphony of tennis, on the brink of yet another decisive tiebreaker.

And what a spectacle it offered! Incredible rallies, unbelievable passing shots, aces, volleys, massive forehands, stylish backhands... Emotionally charged yet exhausting to witness, one can only imagine the strain on

---

[5] In tennis, as a general rule, when the game score stands at 6–6, one more game is played to determine the winner of the set. This game, called tiebreaker, is won by the first player to get 7 points, if there is a winning margin of 2 points. If the score is tied at 6 points all, the tiebreak continues and can't be won on the subsequent point (7–6 or 6–7), as neither player will be two points ahead. Hence, a tiebreaker could go on for long, until one player wins by a score of 18–16 points, for instance.

the players themselves.

As the game score reached 6–6, the tension peaked, promising drama in the tiebreaker—either Nadal's triumph, or Federer's resurrection by prolonging the match into a fifth and deciding set.

This second tiebreaker is lauded by pundits as one of the most extraordinary ever. Nadal initially took a lead of 5–2 points in the breaker and stood on the cusp of clinching the Wimbledon title with his next two serves.

However, a double fault and a netted backhand from Nadal gave Federer a breather, 5–4.

Federer served and won the next two points, 5–6.

Nadal served, saving a set point, 6–6. He then earned his first match point, bringing the score at 7–6. However, he couldn't return Federer's serve.

Tied at 7–7, we jumped as Nadal unleashed a seemingly impossible forehand down the line past Federer.

The score was 8–7, and it marked the second match point for Nadal. The first on Nadal's serve!

Yet, the Swiss maestro responded heroically, countering the Spaniard's serve with one of the most legendary single-handed backhands in tennis history.

Presently, tied at 8–8, Roger Federer had saved two

match points in the fourth set. I don't wish to recall the blasphemies we uttered when Federer won the next two points to claim the fourth set, amidst the thunderous roar of the crowd.

Final tally in the tiebreaker: 10–8 for Federer.

Hence, a fifth and deciding set was in the making. After three and a half hours battling between victory and defeat, Nadal and Federer stood at a crucial juncture, facing both Triumph and Disaster.

For Roger Federer, it was a moment to culminate a historic comeback. For Rafael Nadal, it meant starting anew, having squandered all his earlier lead. It was disheartening to come so close to your goal, only to have it taken away.

Both players were circumambulating the verses of Rudyard Kipling. Now, it was time to rely on the poet:

If you can make one heap of all your winnings
And risk it on one turn of pitch-and-toss,
And lose, and start again at your beginnings
And never breathe a word about your loss.

If you can force your heart and nerve and sinew
To serve your turn long after they are gone,
And so hold on when there is nothing in you
Except the Will which says to them: 'Hold on!'

19:30

"I'll be damned, Frank!"

No, these weren't the exact words Sergio used when Nadal lost the fourth set tiebreaker, missing two match points that appeared as a once-in-a-lifetime opportunity. They had been considerably worse—this is only a sanitised rendition, approved for publication.

The situation was critical for Nadal, at present. It demanded incredible mental resilience and force.

Who would have bet a penny on him in those dire moments? Losing the last two sets and throwing away two match points, one of them on serve, against the ATP World No. 1 player, felt like a dagger to the heart.

It was obvious that the momentum favoured the Swiss.

Now, Federer's fans cheered much louder than

Nadal's, intoxicated with euphoria. Our slogan, "In Nadal we trust!" had transformed into resignation, as seen in Sergio's downcast and sunken face, and my own apathetic demeanour.

The tension was thick in the air.

Nonetheless, to our relief and the surprise of us doubters, Rafael Nadal didn't give up in the fifth set, playing on as if unaffected by the previous circumstances.

The match went on. At the peak of equality, it was again interrupted by rain, with the fifth-set score tied at 2–2, deuce.

19:50

There was a general sense of despair upon witnessing the return of the rain—or rather, drizzle, a more accurate description.

"Keep calm, Sergio" said I, "I'm sure the dark clouds won't stick around."

But as if nature sought to contradict my assurance, rain fell even more obstinately.

I hereby declare that amidst the thousands of fans

gathered on the hill, not a single kind word escaped their lips. Instead, there was a chorale of insults in unison.

"I don't have a day off tomorrow! I'm off on Tuesday, Frank."

I didn't have Monday off either.

"It can't be happening; it just can't be!"

That was me grumbling, my complaints directed at both the rain and the fact that Nadal had missed a historic opportunity.

"Well, let's think for a moment," said Sergio, "if they adjourn the match, I'd need it to rain cats and dogs tomorrow. You know what I mean? Black skies, thunder roaring, lightning flashing, rain all day long."

This way, he could head to Wimbledon on Tuesday to watch the final's deciding set. That was his hypothetical scenario.

"Sergio, let's be realistic," said I, "tomorrow, I'll probably have lunch late. I'll take my break at 2 p.m. to watch the match on TV when it restarts."

Our conversation carried on for a bit longer, until we were enveloped in silence and contemplation, doubtful if the rain would ever cease.

20:15

We felt shivers, not just from nerves but also from the chill that crept in as evening descended. Sitting idly made the cold more palpable, and a blanket would have been welcome.

Thankfully, the match resumed.

Roger Federer came back to serve with full force. Right away, he fired two aces, and swiftly brought the score to 3–2, with Federer in the lead.

At that moment, if we had been told that Nadal would win that fifth set in near darkness, we wouldn't have believed it. Perhaps the only one who believed in the victory of the Balearic slinger—excuse me, tennis player—was Rafael Nadal himself, and his coach Toni Nadal.

Regardless, I ought to highlight the quality of this deciding set. For a tennis fan, it was the zenith, going beyond any personal preferences or patriotisms. The mental fight was also brutal, as intense as the physical one, if not more so.

At 5–5 in the fifth set, the match remained on a knife's

edge, with both players refusing to yield.

The light was fading, making the chalk lines on the grass barely discernible.

Roger Federer got on the brink of victory a couple of times, finding himself just two points shy of clinching his sixth consecutive Wimbledon crown.

However, Nadal persevered, holding onto his serve and eventually breaking Federer's serve in the 15th game, setting the score at 8–7.

It all came to an end then, when Nadal appeared to decipher the Matrix, halting time and space, propelling Federer's last forehand to the net with quantum telepathy, winning 9–7 in the fifth.[6]

21:15

"Game, set and match, Nadal," said the umpire Pascal Maria, ceremoniously, "three sets to two. 6–4, 6–4, 6–7,

---

[6] Please be aware that at that time, the final set did not have a tiebreaker, requiring a two-game advantage instead. However, this regulation has since been amended, and Wimbledon now has implemented a tiebreaker in the fifth set.

6–7, 9–7."

It was dark in Henman Hill. All the tension had come to an end as the cold dissipated amidst jumps and resounding applause.

Rafael Nadal lay on the Wimbledon grass, victorious, tears streaming down his face in disbelief, suddenly grasping the magnitude of the moment.

He promptly got to his feet and clambered up to hug his family members, coaches, and friends. Then, skipping all protocols, he proceeded to walk over the commentary box roof to shake hands with the Spanish royals.

Speaking of royalty, it seemed as though a mighty Balearic warrior had just wielded King Arthur's sword on the hills of Wimbledon, a marriage of British and Spanish folklore. Actually, it's worth noting that Robert Graves hinted at Mallorca as one of the possible locations of Avalon.

Later on, some commentators argued that, due to darkness, the match should have been stopped before its ending. But that might have resulted in a titanic anti-climax.

Additionally, it could have led to chaos in London. The underground trains would have been further overwhelmed on a Monday, and some spectators might have had to cancel their flights and seek accommodation in hotels, amongst other inconveniences.

In any case, it was all over now.

Rafael Nadal had emerged victorious, and possibly the only reasonable discussion was whether they should have awarded a trophy to each of them, based on merit.

22:00

As we hurried to catch the tube, we made some phone calls to explain what we just witnessed. Social media was still in its infancy, and there wasn't much left to do or post about the experience.

I opted to prepare a lengthy mail to my family and friends, which served as the basis for this book. Sergio also managed to capture the winning point with his camera, but unfortunately, the quality wasn't good due to the darkness, the jumping, and the struggle to keep from slipping on the damp Henman Hill.

Now, the adventure was coming to an end with this last

tube ride, filled with Wimbledon spectators enthusiastically discussing the match.

I overheard their conversation for a while. There lingered a collective sense of having witnessed a historic duel, and some amongst them were fortunate to have had the opportunity to observe the match directly from the Centre Court, the cathedral of tennis.

Afterwards, I reflected on some words about victory and constancy, which this dramatic contest had brought to mind:

To fight each time and win; above the tallness reigning.

And it's worth emphasizing that this isn't an allusion to Kipling's "If—," but rather a line from "The Pine of Formentor," written by my collateral relative, the poet Miquel Costa i Llobera.[7]

Beyond witnessing victory, I daresay we were equally blessed to witness the spectacle unfold within the confines of Wimbledon's grounds, even without being in the Centre Court.

The goddess Fortuna tends to favour those who seek

---

[7] Poem translated from the Catalan by the author of this book.

her, and she herself seems more valuable than Victory—which is often hollow and vain. Hence, fortunate those who witnessed this sublime match, regardless of its outcome, as both players battled and encountered Triumph and Disaster.

Picture: Henman Hill, near No. 1 Court, Wimbledon

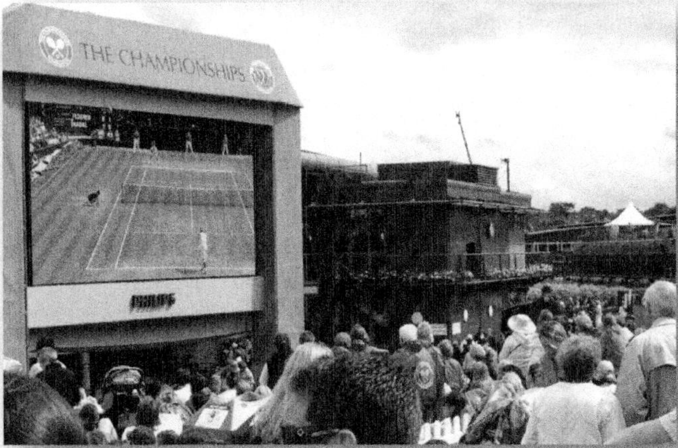
THE CHAMPIONSHIPS
PHILIPS

AFTERWORD

In the annals of tennis history, the 2008 Wimbledon Championships Men's Singles final stands out as the consummate display. Whilst labelling it as the greatest tennis match of all time is subjective and open to debate, this idea didn't originate from the author's imagination.

In fact, John McEnroe, the American pundit and former tennis player who at the time bore witness to the game, stated afterwards that it was: "The greatest match I've ever seen."

Meanwhile, his arch-rival Björn Borg, the Swedish former World No. 1, who had watched the match from the Royal Box, remarked, "That's the best tennis match

I've ever seen in my life. I was just happy to be there, to be part of that final. You cannot see a better tennis match."

Even Roger Federer himself, half-jokingly, shared his viewpoint years later: "Some call it the greatest match of all time. Okay, all respect to Rafa, but I think it would have been way better if I had won..."

Lasting 4 hours and 48 minutes, and without taking into account the rain delays that only heightened the sense of supernatural drama, the final stands as a testament to the sport's popularity and its beauty.

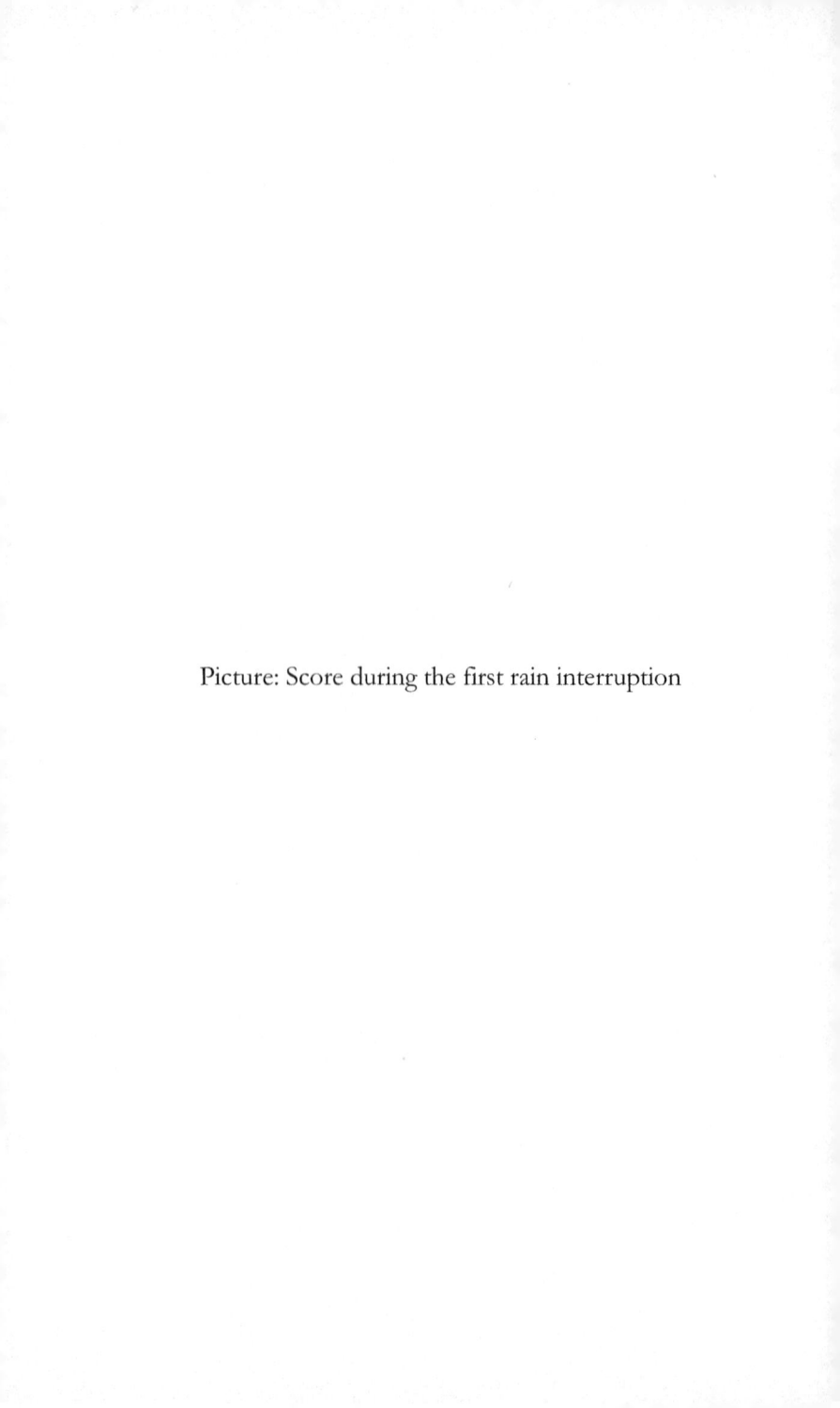

Picture: Score during the first rain interruption

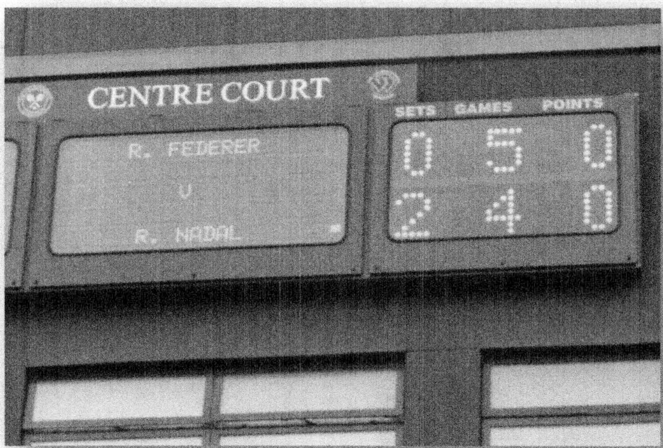
CENTRE COURT
R. FEDERER
V
R. NADAL
SETS GAMES POINTS
0 5 0
2 4 0

ABOUT THE AUTHOR

Frank Z. Llobera is a poet, writer, and translator. He translates between English and Catalan, as well as between English and Spanish, and writes prose and poetry. He was longlisted in the 2021-22 John Dryden Translation Competition of the British Comparative Literature Association for his translation of Miquel Costa i Llobera's "Ode to Horace," and was recently a runner-up in the 2023-24 Poetry Contest in Olot, Catalonia. He published an annotated English translation of the work "The Pine of Formentor" by Costa i Llobera, and is also the founder of @zetapoetry.

@ZETAPOETRY

FINIS CORONAT OPUS

ORDER

MATCH 1

R. FEDERER	v	R. NADAL
H. KONTINEN	v	G. DIMITROV
B. HERCOG / MOORE	v	Miss L. HOLLAND / Miss S. PE...

Printed in Great Britain
by Amazon